D1194608

The Haunted

HARBINGERS 2

Frank Peretti

Angela Hunt, Bill Myers and Alton Gansky

FRANK PERETTI

Published by Amaris Media International.

Copyright © 2015 Frank Peretti

Cover Design: Angela Hunt

Photo © *elenaburn—Fotolia.com*

ISBN: 0692385851
ISBN-13: 978-0692385852

For more information, visit us on Facebook:
https://www.facebook.com/pages/Harbingers/705107309586877

or

www.harbingersseries.com

HARBINGERS

A novella series by

Bill Myers, Frank Peretti, Angela Hunt, and Alton Gansky

In this fast-paced world with all its demands, the four of us wanted to try something new. Instead of the longer novel format, we wanted to write something equally as engaging but that could be read in one or two sittings—on the plane, waiting to pick up the kids from soccer, or as an evening's read.

We also wanted to play. As friends and seasoned novelists, we thought it would be fun to create a game we could participate in together. The rules were simple:

Rule #1
Each of us would write as if we were one of the characters in the series:

Bill Myers would write as Brenda, the street-hustling tattoo artist who sees images of the future.

Frank Peretti would write as the professor, the atheist ex-priest ruled by logic.

Angela Hunt would write as Andi, the professor's brilliant-but-geeky assistant who sees inexplicable patterns.

Alton Gansky would write as Tank, the naïve, big-hearted jock with a surprising connection to a healing power.

Rule #2

Instead of the four of us writing one novella together (we're friends but not crazy), we would write it like a TV series. There would be an overarching story line into which we'd plug our individual novellas, with each story written from our character's point of view.

Bill's first novella, *The Call*, sets the stage. It will be followed by Frank's, *The Haunted*, Angela's *The Sentinels*, and Alton's *The Girl*. And if we keep having fun, we'll begin a second round and so on until other demands pull us away or, as in TV, we get cancelled.

There you have it. We hope you'll find these as entertaining in the reading as we did in the writing.

Bill, Frank, Angie, and Al

Chapter 1

Clyde Morris

Clyde Morris looked entirely the part of a wraith: neck tendons tuned like a harp, white hair wild, fogging corneas following unseen demons about the old dining room. "My life, my years, all over. Done! Can't reach them from here, can't change them, no more chances!"

His frumpish wife Nadine could make no sense of his ravings, his clenching and unclenching hands, his rising, pacing, sitting again, his seeing horrible things. She reached across the table to touch him, but drew her hand back—it felt chilled as with frost.

He leaned, nearly lunged over the table, his face

close to hers. "It knows me! It knows all about me!"

From down the hall came the shriek of door hinges. Clyde's eyes rolled toward the sound, his veiny face contorted. A wind rustled the curtains, fluttered a newspaper, swung the chandelier so it jingled.

Clyde stood and the wind hit him broadside, pushing him toward the hall.

"Clyde!"

He reached across the space between them but the wind, roaring, carried him down the hall along with cushions, newspapers, the tablecloth.

A doorway in the hall, glowing furnace red, pulled him. He craned forward to fight it, stumbled, grappled, and slid backward toward it.

The doorway sucked him in like a dust particle. A high-pitched scream faded into infinite distance until cut off when the door slammed shut.

The wind stopped. The newspaper pages settled to the floor. A doily fluttered down like a snowflake. The chandelier jingled through two diminishing swings, then stopped jingling and hung still.

Now the only sound was the wailing of the widow, flung to the floor in the old Victorian house.

Chapter 2

The Phenomenon

When A. J. Van Epps first called to relate what had happened—or allegedly happened—to crusty old Clyde Morris, I fidgeted, perused lecture notes, indulged him. Why would a learned academic and researcher like Van Epps trouble himself—and now me—with a campfire tale too easily debunked to warrant the effort? The largely one-sided conversation took a feeble turn toward interesting only when I discerned in Van Epps' voice a tone of dread so unlike him, and it was after that hook was set that he sprang his proposal: would I come and assist in the investigation, would I help him regain his objectivity, would I lend my knowledge and experience?

Oh yes, exactly what my frayed nerves needed. Being in a near plane crash and hauled into a misadventure in a so-called "Institute for Advanced Psychic Studies," not to mention having my personal and deepest fears vivisected by one and the same, were a sleepy, monotonous ordeal. I needed the change.

Besides . . .

We were old friends and associates. I would be lecturing at Evergreen State College in the Puget Sound area in the next few days. Of course I could afford a side trip to help him look into the matter. I agreed to come—and kicked myself the moment I ended the call.

McKinney here. Dr. James McKinney, sixty, professor of philosophy and comparative religions, emeritus, at large, published, and so on and so forth. Generally, a scholar of religious claims and systems, but specifically, a skeptic, and it is to that last title I devote the most attention. This, I trust, lends explanation for why I and Andrea Goldstein, my young assistant, drove our rental car through the meandering and sloping village of Port Avalon and located the quaint Victorian residence of Dr. A.J. Van Epps.

Van Epps, thinner and grayer than I remembered, took our coats, then expended no more than a minute or two on greetings and how-are-yous before he led us to his kitchen table and brought up a photograph on his computer: A two-story Victorian home, dull purple, richly detailed, turreted, with covered porch and sleepy front windows.

"My interest, of course, is to ascertain how it works, what empowers it, what measure or means of controlled stimuli will produce predictable results."

Andi and I studied the photo. I saw a house; it was Andi's way to see more, always more, which was one reason I took her along.

"Seven panels in the door," she said. "Each window has seven panes. There are seven front steps."

Not that I appreciated her timing. "Save it for later," I advised, then asked Van Epps, "So this is a house here in town?"

Van Epps inserted an artful pause before answering, "Sometimes."

This whole affair was ludicrous enough. "A.J., I'm not known for my patience."

"Check out the landmarks: This tree with the large knot; this fire hydrant; this seam in the street." He arrow-keyed to a second photograph, what one would call a vacant lot: some brush, some trees, nothing else . . . save for the same knotted tree, fire hydrant, and seam in the street in front. "I took this soon after the first. The house was there, and then it wasn't."

I didn't stifle an irritated sigh. "If I may—just to cover the obvious—these photos are digital."

He sighed back. "I didn't alter them. No Photoshop."

"And you've presented them in the order you took them?"

"Yes."

"So I'm to take you seriously?"

He leaned back and held my gaze with his own. "I've found something, James, something atypical. As you'll observe, Port Avalon is one of those . . .

alternative kinds of town that attract all brands of superstition, so the locals have their legends about it, how it's a harbinger of death, how it knows you, follows you . . . " With an unbecoming cryptic note he added, "Takes you."

I rubbed my eyes, mostly to buy time. I was at a loss.

"I came to Port Avalon with the specific objective of encountering this House in order to study it, know it. I saw it for myself a month ago, even before the incident with Clyde Morris, and yes, there is *something* about it that would trigger such legends, so I have to ask, what is it really? And can we control it, maybe harness whatever powers it?"

"Harness? What are you talking about?"

He fidgeted, composing an answer. "I and some friends are interested in occult power—not as occult power, you understand, but as . . . power. Power that could be useful."

"Friends?"

"Investors, shall we say."

I knew he wouldn't go any further into it. Maybe another time. "A. J., if you want me to bring balance to this—"

"Absolutely! I can see the handwriting on the wall, this is no plaything."

"Then I'll be skeptical. Digital photographs? Legends? To waste my time is to insult me. Show me evidence beyond this."

"There's Nadine, Clyde Morris' widow. You should hear her account. She was there, in the House, when it took him."

I rose deliberately. "Then we'll go there now."

The closet door was locked.

"Other door," Van Epps said.

I found the closet, grabbed and put on my coat. Andi threw hers on.

"There's more," said Van Epps.

It was my role to get him on track and I persisted. I recognized his favorite jacket in the front closet: fine leather, and a distinctive smell. I grabbed it and held it out to him.

With his eyes turned away from his computer, he swiveled it to show us another photo, that of a ghostly old man with glassy eyes and hunched shoulders glaring at the camera. The lighting was rather dim, the photo taken outdoors at dusk or later. "Clyde Morris."

I would have none of the chill I felt and shook it off. Andi showed the same chill plainly. "He could have been dead already." I was being sarcastic.

"He was," said Van Epps. "He died a week before I took this."

Chapter 3

Encounters

Nadine Morris took one look at Van Epps' photo of the House and looked away, tears once again filling her reddened eyes. She nodded yes, and Van Epps gave me a look.

"And where was it?" he asked her.

We were sitting in her small, long-dated living room. She pointed through her front window at the woods across the street. "It was right there, like it was waiting, like it was watching me."

Andi immediately pointed out the knotty tree, fire hydrant, and concrete seam.

I had to look around Andi's explosive red hair—

like a sea urchin with a perm—but I expected as much.

Nadine continued, "And then it was here. It wasn't our house anymore, it was *that* house, and I was sitting in it and . . ." She trembled. "There was Clyde, sitting in the dining room." She broke into a whimper. "But he was only a spirit. His time had come."

"He'd passed away a week before—" Van Epps began.

I cut him off. "I want to hear it from her."

"At Daisy Meadows," she said. "The assisted living facility. He died in his sleep. But the House wouldn't let him rest. It chased his spirit around town until that night when it caught him . . . and sucked him into hell."

Ravings. I ventured a challenge. "How do you know he was sucked into hell?"

"He was a difficult man, wasn't he?" Van Epps asked.

Nadine stiffened. "He didn't mean to hurt me. It was the drink, you know."

"Objectivity! Scientific method!" My voice was raised. It gets that way when people don't think. "You are a researcher, a debunker! What's come over you?"

Van Epps sat hunched and self-protective at his kitchen table while I paced about the room. "I thought it could pertain."

"Whether Clyde Morris was deserving of hell? What bearing could that possibly have on an explainable phenomenon?"

He had to work up an answer. "I was exploring the phenomenon through her point of view."

"You were leading the witness!"

Van Epps and I had had our heated discussions before. I took it in stride when he lashed out, "I came eye to eye with a posthumous manifestation of Clyde Morris! I photographed it! I felt the intensity of it! There *is* a human element here and we have to consider it."

"From an objective base, which you no longer have."

He halted, then raised a hand in surrender. "No. No, I don't. That's why I need you here." He drew a breath, recovering a measure of professionalism. "The House exerts a strong effect on the human psyche, and I could be a case in point. When it first appeared, I truly felt it was looking into me as if it knew me. As if—note this—it knew my sins. And that look I got from Clyde Morris . . . "

I sat next to him. "Religious guilt?"

He smiled, nodded. "I'm sure you can relate."

"Of course." Van Epps knew of my ill-fated days in the priesthood, and he'd shared a little of his Sunday school background. "I've found a good dose of reason and logic can make it go away . . . usually."

"And the power of suggestion can bring it back. In this town there's plenty of that."

I rose. "Which, if I'm to be clinical, I need to apprise. Andi, get online, find out if there's any precedent for what we're seeing here, any other cases of a house appearing and disappearing and . . . holding people morally accountable." I looked at Van Epps. "Fair assessment?"

He nodded, chagrined.

"Want to come along?"

"No. I'll write up what we have so far. That should

clear my system of . . . whatever this is."

"Good enough."

Port Avalon was a small town nestled on the forested hillsides above Puget Sound. I drove less than four minutes to reach the town center, and could surmise from the boats, docks, and harbor the town's origins as a fishing village.

That, I guessed, had to be before the sixties and the influx ever afterward of the mystical set who favored seclusion, nature, and the nearness of the sea. Such mundane businesses as an Ace Hardware, a pharmacy, and a floral shop held precious ground amid a disproportionate measure of Eastern, animist, and mystical enterprises: tarot readers, fortune tellers, psychic healers, shamans, meditation centers and pagan temples. Here the objects of worship were goddesses, ascended masters, Mother Earth, any growing thing.

I walked about, "fishing" for data and beginning to understand Van Epps' conundrum. Port Avalon was saturated with the human need for explanation, for an answer to the question *Why*, for a basis of knowing good and evil or even the existence of such things. I had long ago established to my comfort that such cosmic questions developed only from our need for survival and holding our societies together, but as this town demonstrated, those who could accept morality as a matter of utility and not "truth" were few, and the pervasive norms of this place could easily aggravate the old "pang of conscience." Poor Van Epps. This place was getting to him.

And getting to me as well, I thought, halting on the sidewalk. Across the street I saw what an unprepared mind could take to be a cosmic coincidence.

There, engaged in conversation with the gypsy-costumed proprietor of "Earthsong's Psychic Readings," was the brusque and urbanesque tattoo artist, Brenda . . .

I'd forgotten her last name and that was fine with me, but her dreadlocks and slinking posture were unmistakable.

A plague on this town! In that moment I nearly believed some game master somewhere was moving us about like chess pieces. It was more than enough that she'd been on the same plane Andi and I took to Seattle, and not only she, but the wide-eyed giant we called Tank, and all by happenstance. Yes, I argued with myself—and the town—happenstance, even if Tank should show up in Port Avalon as well.

Perish the thought. The last time I, Andi, the tattooist, and the giant were lumped together, it was to invade that ridiculous Institute, trespassing, vandalizing, and resorting to pointless acts of heroism. Heroism! Now there was another conundrum: if in this random and purposeless universe there was no basis for right and wrong, how could there be any point to heroism?

I deliberately gave my head a shake to cast off all this tizzy. I thought I would turn away.

If anyone ever attributes my decision to fate, luck, God, or any other capricious power, I will fervently deny it. I was, after all, "fishing," and if the fish might be across the street . . .

I crossed, though it pained me.

"Well—" was as far as my greeting went before Earthsong got whammy-eyed.

"Ohhh!" she said with serpent-handed histrionics, "you are looking for someone!" She reeked of incense and her bracelets jangled. It was strictly carnival. "Would you like to know more?"

Brenda—I recalled her last name was Barnick—seemed pleasantly surprised at the sight of me. "Oh, this is the guy! I was—"

"Yes," I said. "I'd like to know more, anything you have to say."

Brenda made a face that telegraphed *are you putting me on?*

I'd been struck in that moment by another coincidence. I had a fish on the line, tugging. I wanted to land it.

Chapter 4

Earthsong

I felt in violation of my own precepts, sitting in Earthsong's mystical, candlelit parlor, listening raptly as she went through a well-rehearsed spiel. Yes, the crystal ball was there in the center of the table; the incense was burning and tainting everything, including ourselves; a carved, ruby-eyed raven perched above our heads lending mood and . . . vibration? Brenda shot me many a sideways glance through the proceedings, but I suggested by my own behavior the role she should play: gullible, enraptured. She fell into it quite well.

"I see . . . a child!" said Earthsong, waving her

fingers over the crystal ball. "Young . . . innocent . . . blond hair. Strangely silent." She then sneered. "Ha! He is thought to have a gift, but next to me, he is nothing! He knows nothing of the real powers! It was a waste to consult him! A waste!"

I was not experienced in discerning drug-affected behavior, but I had to suspect she was high on something. I would definitely consult the streetwise Brenda afterward.

The fortune teller continued. "He was a prisoner, but broke his bonds and is free! And now . . . " She made eye contact for effect. "You seek him!"

"And where is he?" Brenda asked.

Role playing? At least it spurred the conversation.

"This is the cry of the powers! Where is he? Where is he?" Earthsong consulted her crystal ball. "Ask the House. The House will know. The House . . . "

From there she went into a fit, something she must have learned by watching the channelers on television in the eighties. We got nothing more from her except the amount of her fee: Twenty dollars.

Brenda and I made our way up the sidewalk, chained to each other by curiosity.

"What the devil are you doing here?" I demanded.

"What are *you* doing here?"

I explained Van Epps' invitation, meaning I had to detail the bizarre reasons as well.

She returned my favor, explaining, "Got an invitation, plane ticket and everything, from a tattoo agent in Seattle, something about starting a franchise. Called himself a tattoo *brokerage*! That should have been a clue right there. It was a rip-off. They get me the work and take a percentage, but the fine print says

I can only work through them and they own my designs. So screw 'em, but thanks for the free ride."

"But what are you doing *here*?"

"Don't get your boxers in a wad. I saw a poster in the agent's lobby, said you were lecturing at Evergreen State. I said, 'Hey, what're you guys doing plugging a don't-believe-in-nothing guy like this?' The guy tears the poster off the wall and throws it in the fireplace."

I could see her watching it in her mind's eye.

"I saw you burning, curling up, going to ashes. I called Evergreen—what's that face for? Yeah, I called 'em and they said you were coming up here to see a friend."

"You came here because somebody burned a poster of me?"

"Listen, I'd need more than that to trouble myself over you." She dug in her shoulder bag and brought out a sketch pad. "I saw *this* right after that."

She showed me her drawing of a snaky logo with scaly lettering: Psychic Readings, Fortunes Told. We both looked back to verify the same logo above Earthsong's front door.

"You saw this on the bulletin board?"

She sniffed her impatience and pointed to her head. "In here, my man. I see things in here and I draw them. That's why I stopped there to talk to the lady. I said, 'Hey, I'm trying to find somebody,' and right then, there you were. Now you do what you want with it, but that's what happened."

"So that's how she got the idea we were looking for someone . . . " I mused. "Except I wasn't. Not you, not the little blond kid." I chuckled. "She couldn't have been further off."

"So why'd you spend the twenty bucks?"

We'd come to my car. I nodded to the passenger door. "Let's have a chat."

Inside, I cautioned her to secrecy and continued. "It seems my friend Van Epps has a close relationship with that lady. The moment I reached her front door I caught the odor of her incense—a smell that permeates Van Epps' leather jacket. He's been to her place on a regular basis."

"Did you see the needle tracks on her arms?"

"I was going to ask you—"

"She was high. Heroin. I've seen it."

"High and careless. Being a charlatan, she guessed wrong and told us somebody else's fortune. But the information is likely true: somebody's looking for a child—"

"I've seen the kid."

"—and I have to wonder what Van Epps knows about it."

"Are we talking or just you?"

"Sorry?"

"I've seen that kid."

I had to clarify. "Where?"

She indicated her head again.

"I suppose you have a drawing?"

"Not on me."

"Hmph."

"It's on Tank's arm. A little blond kid, standing there with the rest of us."

We were going over a cliff. I applied some brakes.

"Let's categorize what we have. You claim to be here following information gained through some kind of psychic means—"

"No I don't!"

"Whatever, all right? Just for now?"

"I don't do trances and I don't trip out . . . and I don't have a freaky carved raven!"

"Granted. But let's put all that here in this category—" I indicated a small corral with my hands, then indicated another beside the first—"and another category here, for data gathered the old fashioned way, through observation."

She was either bored or miffed, looking elsewhere.

I proceeded anyway. "In the second category, Earthsong is tied to Van Epps, and that being the case, he may know something about this child, something he's chosen not to talk about."

She looked at me again. "She's jealous of the kid, you know that."

I nodded. "He supposedly has a gift she went out of her way to discredit."

"So he's a threat, so he's real."

"I agree."

"So what about the rest of it? The kid in prison and breaking out and somebody wondering where he is . . . "

"And the House knowing . . . " We now had a bag of pieces that didn't connect. "I'll have a word with Van Epps about it, if only to get his reaction." Then, wanting data first and accepting explanation later, I added, "In the meantime, let me know if you see any more pictures."

She gave me a look.

"No, please do."

Chapter 5

Gustav Svensson

Van Epps disappointed me—not for lack of information I could at least infer, but for lack of honesty with me, his old compatriot in skepticism.

He asked me about my walk through the town. I recounted my impressions and introduced Brenda. He asked if we'd noticed the overburden of mystics and charlatans, and of course we had.

"Places like . . . Earthsong's Psychic Readings," he said with a sardonic wag of his head. "So typical."

How notable that he brought up the fortuneteller without my mentioning her. I pursued it. "We gave her a try, as a matter of fact. She put on quite a show."

He sneered, he scoffed, he chided me for wasting my time and money.

"She spoke of a missing child," I said with a mockery to match his. "Obviously, a 'reading' that had nothing to do with us."

He laughed along with me, but drummed his fingers nervously and would not dwell on the subject.

From there, things went into a limbo that became more and more constricting. We went to several homes around the neighborhood and town, but the reactions we got were as Van Epps predicted from his own experience: No one talked about the House.

After that, a day passed, then another, and we became like survivors in a lifeboat, stuck in close proximity with nowhere else to go. Van Epps and I fell into quarrels over old information when we weren't exhausting each other in protracted academic discussions. His house was sizable enough for his guests, but not sizable enough to prevent friction between myself and the two women.

Andi, lacking something to do, began jabbering about patterns: The dimensions of the cupboard doors were golden rectangles, the tea kettle played a continuous tone progressing through ten degrees of the scale and ending on an accidental, the pattern of the living room carpet repeated every forty-eight inches, which was the same number of flowers in the pattern multiplied by four, so there had to be more twelves or multiples of twelve somewhere. There was no turning her off.

Brenda, always edgy, wandered, explored, got to know some people, but the idleness weighed upon her and she simply could not find something to like.

She didn't like the town, she didn't like the house, she didn't care for Van Epps and of course, she could not accommodate herself to me—a mutual feeling I had no incentive to correct.

And all along, Van Epps kept pressing us. "It'll show up again. Count on it. You'll see."

Then came October 6th. The day held no significance for me, but for Andi, it was the number six, the number the Institute seemed so fond of, which was divisible into twelve, which constituted the pattern she was waiting for. "It's the sixth! I think we're going to get something today!"

I got out of the house—alone. That was the point.

I walked the same loop around the neighborhood, past the same trees, hedges, yards, and yapping dogs I'd memorized by now, vexed by the monotony, the sameness, the cyclical repetition . . .

Until I noticed a different sensation: beneath my vexation, a sense of gloom moved in like a mood swing on a cloudy day; feelings associated with the memory of a woman I could not have . . . shadows of regret . . . anger . . . the day I tore off my clerical collar.

Blast! I had long ago buried all such issues. It had to be the town, the idleness, and now my being exiled as it were, a solitary soul on an empty sidewalk in a strange town. I dashed the memories from my mind—

And felt a sense of foreboding as if being followed. Watched.

I looked about. No one behind me—

The moment my eyes came forward, I saw only twenty feet away . . . him? It? I will use the term *specter* to convey the appearance of the man and, I admit, the chill, the danger I felt. He was motionless, like a post. His eyes, pasted over like those of a dead animal, were locked on me. How he could make such an instant appearance and from where, I could not tell.

He was dressed like an aged mariner: old slicker, drooping hat, work boots. His complexion was cold and gray, and he was dripping wet, standing in a puddle of water though it was a rainless day.

He took a step toward me, and then another, the grim expression steady as a mask. Intuitively, I considered my size and strength and so resolved to stand my ground. The boots squished and left wet footprints on the street. The slicker dripped as if being rained upon.

Now he seemed he would move by me, so I stepped aside. He passed by, his pasty eyes probing me, and it had to have been Van Epps' prior description that made me feel he was looking into me, knew me, knew my sins.

The specter's back was to me now. I fumbled for my cell phone to snap a photo. Even as I composed the picture, he stopped and looked back. Click. A photo I might fear from that day.

What? The man gave his head a little jerk as if to say, *Come this way.*

I followed him at a distance even as I swiped and tapped my phone to raise Andi's number. When she answered, I found myself whispering. "Come quickly, all of you."

Oh, the frustration!

"Come where?" she said. "Where are you?"

Somewhere in Port Avalon, blast it! "I don't know the street name. I'm near the big white house with the black mutt."

"Well where's that?"

I came to a street sign. "Mossyrock." The man kept walking around a corner, up a hill. "Make that 48th."

"Forty-eight!" she exclaimed.

I hated how she could make me curse, especially to her. "Do not start, Andi! Just get down here!"

She indicated that Van Epps knew where I was. I tapped off and holstered the phone.

The specter rounded a wooded corner and went out of sight. I ran to catch sight of him again.

There he was, relentlessly walking, squishing, dripping.

And just beyond him, at the end of the street where, I'm sure, nothing but woods had been, was a house. Two-story Victorian, dull purple, richly detailed, turreted, with covered porch and sleepy front windows.

Chapter 6

The House

The "posthumous manifestation" of whoever this was seemed in no hurry. Rather, he stepped and squished up the seven steps to the front porch of the House, turned, looked at me, then waited until the others arrived.

Andi and Brenda spilled out of Van Epps' car. "Who is it?" "What is it?" Then they stood next to me and gawked.

"Looks like an old fisherman," Andi observed.

Brenda chose to respond by invoking the sanctity of excrement.

I was relieved that they saw it too.

Van Epps remained in his car, hiding, it seemed, behind the steering wheel even as the apparition stared at him with much the same expression as Clyde Morris had in that photo. A pattern there, but now I could relate.

The specter scanned us as if taking attendance. The front door opened by itself. He went inside and the door closed with a creak and a clunk.

Only then did Van Epps scramble from his car with a video camera and tripod. "See? I told you! There it is, right in front of you!"

"Looks real enough," said Andi. "Different landmarks, though. No knotty tree or fire hydrant. Not this time."

Emotions were running high, mine included. I dared not be fooled. I studied the House, cautious to sort reality from illusion, scanning the lines of the walls, gables, roof. The windows drew my gaze and I found myself looking the House in the eyes. Van Epps' observation was not unfounded, though subjective, as mine was at that moment: I couldn't shake the impression that the House was staring me down, just like the old fisherman. I couldn't ask the ladies what they might be feeling lest I suggest the idea to them. I tried moving from side to side. Still, the gaze of the windows followed me. *I know all about you*, said the House. *I know all about you.*

By now, word had filtered through the town. People showed up in little clusters, keeping their distance, gawking, taking pictures with their cell phones.

It was Gustav, someone said. Gustav Svensson. They tossed the name around, repeated it, passed it from one to another.

I listened. I counted and recorded faces, trying not to stare too long at a man and woman stationed behind the others. I may have seen them before, but impressions were questionable at the moment.

Brenda and Andi were looking to me for the next move. I looked at Van Epps. He was behind a tree with the camera.

"Shall we have a closer look?" I asked.

"Yes, by all means," he answered. "Go ahead. I'll keep recording."

"Recording what?"

"It might move again! It might—we need a record."

I looked at the ladies. "Shall we?"

Brenda, clearly unsettled, swore again. I couldn't have said it better.

It was getting dark, which seemed to be a cue for the crowd. They began to back away, then disperse in ones and twos.

A glow appeared in an upstairs window and there were gasps from those remaining—and from Andi.

"Hey," said Brenda. "Somebody's home."

"Yeah," said Andi, "the dead guy."

"Ghosts don't need lights."

Van Epps called from behind the tree. "We need data. You should go inside and check around. I'll keep the camera going in case something happens."

Reading Van Epps' voice and body, I agreed. "Yes. I think you should stay out here."

The walkway was real, as were the front steps, as was the porch. Brenda thumped on a porch post and gave a little shrug. Andi was counting things: the lap siding, the light fixtures, the—

"Hey," she said, "there's no house number!"

She could even get excited about the lack of something.

Since the House was real enough, I thought I should try a real knock on the door. No answer. I knocked two more times, but still no answer. I tried the door. Locked. Brenda had to try the door for herself. Still locked.

The daylight was fading to a steely gray. I led the way around the House while we could still see the details: concrete foundation embedded in the ground; small yard with grass a bit shaggy. Planting beds, but flowers withering this time of year; moss growing on the roof; some paint peeling.

We continued to circle, breathing easier. For a phantasm, the House was so normal as to be disappointing—

Until we caught a glimpse of something or someone moving around the corner toward the front of the House and Andi, her nerves wound tight, screamed. I found a windfallen branch on the lawn and picked it up for a weapon—which had to look silly, more like I wanted to build a campfire than assail an enemy. Nevertheless, the ladies followed close behind as I, their masculine protector, wielded my tree branch. We inched our way around the front corner . . .

"Well, howdy!"

We wilted with relief.

"Whatcha guys doing,' buildin' a fire?"

I dropped the branch. It would have been nice if Tank, our gentle giant, *were* an illusion, but of course that was not to be. He was carrying a duffel bag over his shoulder, a traveler just arrived. Brenda and Andi embraced him, their high pitched greetings as pleasant to me as worn brakes: *How'd you get here?*

So this was their new masculine protector, I supposed.

"Hitched a ride. A computer geek was coming right by here on his way to Port Townsend."

"So how'd the interview go?" Andi asked.

Tank was gushing with the news. "Gonna be a dawg! Full scholarship, baby!"

Ah yes. His football scholarship to the University of Washington. A wonderful, happy subject to take up time and distract all of us from the enigma now demanding our attention. So why was he here and not on his way back home?

"Don't tell me," I said. "You had a vision, or God spoke from a cloud, or . . . "

Tank's eyes went mystical. "I . . . received a message!"

Of course. I rolled my eyes.

"Andi called me." He stood there grinning at his own cleverness. The three shared a laugh—at me.

I directed an icy employer's look at Andi, who justified herself. "Calling him was logical, objective, totally pragmatic! Case in point right here."

She looked at Tank and nodded toward the front door. "It's locked."

"So?" he asked. After his neurotransmitters connected he wagged his head. "Eh, I dunno. That's somebody's house, you know?"

Van Epps called from behind the tree, "Just open the door!"

Tank looked for where the voice had come from. "What's he doin' back there?"

"He thinks the place is haunted," Brenda

28

whispered.

Tank's face went blank. "Really?"

"Perhaps you might justify your presence here," I prodded.

Tank acquiesced and went up the front steps with the rest of us in tow. I was about to advise the ladies to give the big fellow some room for safety's sake—

He simply turned the knob and the door creaked open. He gave us a puzzled look. I looked at Brenda and she shrugged back.

"Hello?" Tank called.

Of course, he hadn't been here earlier. He hadn't seen the apparition or heard all the background. He walked right in as if his mother lived there. Still nursing our trepidations, we followed.

Chapter 7

Explorations

We couldn't find a light switch anywhere and the daylight coming through the windows was quickly fading. Andi got out her cell phone and used the flashlight feature to produce a sharp beam she could play about.

So what were we expecting? A decaying netherworld draped in cobwebs? A flurry of frightened bats and ghostly glows against the walls? Trapdoors, secret passages, mysterious wailings in the dark? As our eyes adjusted to the dim light and Andi helped with her cell phone, we found ourselves in a residence clean and furnished as if the housekeepers had just left and the owners were due home any minute. We could admire the entry way with its hall tree and grandfather clock; the ascending staircase with finely turned balusters and railing; the living room, furnished in Victorian style, and beyond that, the formal dining room with high-backed upholstered chairs, eight place settings, and jeweled chandelier. The place was benign, dignified, even welcoming.

So what the deuce caused this trembling in my hands, this animal sense of being cornered? Power of suggestion? The eerie sight of our ghostly guide? Perhaps the darkness and the unknown.

I handed Andi my cell phone. She activated the flashlight while I watched and found out how to do it—learning new technology from her was becoming a routine with me. Brenda and Tank got the same idea, and soon we were moving about like techno-fireflies, pinpoints of light casting stark shadows. I held my phone in both hands to steady the shaking, angry at the dread I couldn't qualm.

A door clicked and swung open in the hallway. I heard a toilet flush. "Toilet works," Andi reported.

Well. Something normal. I was grateful.

The next door she checked refused to open, apparently locked, but I stopped her from asking Tank to try it. Maybe it was the House's effect on me, but I felt such a barrier should be honored. We were being invasive as it was.

The floor of the entry way was slippery. I lowered my light to find a trail of drippings and wet boot prints leading toward the stairs. Perhaps only to remain the cold and objective investigator, I reached down, wetted my fingertip in the drippings and put the sample to my tongue.

Seawater.

Brenda called from the kitchen. We gathered there like bees to a hive, lights hovering, snooping.

On the kitchen table were a jar of jam, one of peanut butter, a loaf of bread, and an uneaten corner of a sandwich left on a plate.

Tank's voice made us all jump. "Hello? Anybody here? Hey, we're your friends, we won't hurt you."

Something bumped somewhere in the House. I looked in each face and got a shrug, a wag—*It wasn't me.*

Brenda shook her dreadlocked head and laughed—at herself and us. "Somebody's living here and we are gonna get busted."

"But it wasn't here before!" said Andi.

"You sure about that?"

I interposed, "May we at least resolve the question of the old fisherman? We all saw him, did we not?"

"Did we *not?*" said Tank. "Yeah, I didn't."

"We do have his boot prints and water dripped on the floor—seawater, by the way—leading up the stairs."

Oh, the pall of doom that fell over Brenda and Andi's faces! As for Tank, for some reason he just wasn't getting it.

It was my idea, so I led. Tank followed me. The ladies followed, but several steps behind. We agreed not to sneak, but to walk benignly up those stairs, calling hello as we went. Our lights went where our eyes went, meaning everywhere, and frantically.

There was no light switch at the top of the stairs and the hallway was an unlit tunnel save for our cellphones. The boot tracks, now dark, wet imprints in the carpet, led to a doorway. I knocked. I called.

There was no answer. I tried the door and it opened.

There was only a dark bedroom on the other side. There was no light switch, and we found soon enough there was no occupant.

"But isn't this where the light was on?" Brenda wondered.

Andi searched the ceiling with her light. There was no lighting fixture, no lamp in the room. "Well . . . it was a light, but that doesn't mean it was an electric light . . ."

"Don't, don't do that."

Shining my cell phone and feeling with my hand, I carefully traced the boot prints to a wet spot in the center of the room. There, they ended.

"Okay," said Brenda, "Now how about we get out of here?"

I wanted to agree, but Van Epps would be waiting behind his tree wanting data and trusting me to be the unaffected gatherer. "We haven't learned anything."

Andi tapped off her light. "Save your batteries."

Our phones winked out and despite my efforts, I felt the dark closing in on me and fear twisting my viscera like a seizure. Blast it! I could turn my phone light back on, but they would ask why; I could explain, but that would plant a suggestion that would skew our observations. It could also make me look like a coward.

"So what now?" Andi asked. Her voice was weak. Perhaps she was feeling the same visceral reaction.

I loathed the answer even as I spoke it. "If we leave for the night, the House may relocate. There are no lights and our phones can only provide so much. We need to go through this place in the light of day." I felt I was delivering a line from an old horror movie:

"We'll have to spend the night."

Chapter 8

During the Night

If I'd been given to flights of imagination, I would have imagined the House expecting our visit. Though it was late September, the House was pleasantly warm; though there were no lights, there was running water and the toilets worked; the bedrooms were fully furnished, the beds made up with fresh linens.

"We are gonna get busted," Brenda moaned.

We laid out a plan, beginning with two escape routes should anything strange occur. There were four upstairs bedrooms; each of us would take a room and stand watch for a two hour slot during the night while the rest slept—assuming any of us could sleep.

We would remain clothed in case we had to make a sudden exit. If anything strange should occur, we were all within shouting distance.

"Any questions?" I asked. There were none.

I advised Van Epps of our plan. While I remained to monitor the camera, he drove home and returned with a chair, an extra coat, and a thermos of coffee. I left him at his station and returned to the House, the front door admitting me without resistance.

We all said good night.

If I may personify, the House had a plan as well. We never saw the morning from inside those confining rooms or that dark hallway. The House saw to it.

My two hours came first. Needless to say, I wasn't sleepy. I found a seafaring novel on the night stand and sat in a comfortable chair to sample it by the light of my cell phone. Less than one chapter in, I found Andi was right regarding cell phones as flashlights— the typical phone cannot last long as a typical flashlight. After one final look around the room I tapped out the light to save the phone's battery.

As I feared, the darkness closed in on me again. My insides tightened like a dishrag being wrung out; I felt like bait awaiting a predator.

Blast this House! Blast this fear, this consuming, irrational phobia! What was the dark but the absence of light, and nothing more? What lurked in that darkness other than a bed, a nightstand, a picture on the wall? Nothing!

I tapped my phone—my hands were shaking so badly it took several tries. At last, the tiny light came on, proving, of course, there was nothing there but a bedroom with its furnishings. I tapped the light off.

Immediately, I knew, I just *knew* that darkness was a living, malevolent thing.

Then the phobia brought delusion. The House could have spoken audibly, the impression was so real. *I know all about you*, said the House. *I know all about you.*

Shades of my church experience: the ever present thumb of God upon the back of me, the insect! I fought to regain mastery. No, I thought, and then I muttered, "*No*, there is nothing here. This is a fiction of my imagination."

Oh? the House seemed to answer.

"You are a lifeless structure of stone and wood," I said, mostly to convince myself. "You have no mind, no plan, and you don't know me!"

I know all about you. I know all about you.

I would not engage this lifeless thing in moral arguments; I would not justify myself to a pernicious phobia! I tapped my cell phone for precious light and locked my eyes on the painting over the bed: sailboats heeling on white-crested waves. Just look at the sailboats, I told myself. Happy. Alive. Tangible. Something real. A tether to sanity.

The light began to dim to a yellow glow, weaker, weaker. I strained to see the painting—

Before my eyes, like black mold growing in time lapse, tiny specks percolated through the wall, widened into patches that widened into areas, surrounded then covered the picture, thickening, ever thickening—toward me.

I suppose it was logic, pragmatism, and yes, my own vanity that kept me in the chair, none of which deterred the phenomenon. It boiled out of the wall, an inky eruption. In the faint orange light from my phone I searched for the picture on the wall—it was inundated, gone. The bed disappeared next, then the nightstand. The *presence* obscured the top of the door, then the top half, filling the room, expanding downward. The closet was nowhere to be seen. As if with a diabolical mind, it saved my little corner for last, swallowing up the space on my right, on my left . . . above me.

The light from my phone went dead.

Chapter 9

Four Messages

I had no thoughts, no theories, nothing left but instinct. I dropped to the floor because it was the only place to go. I rolled, groping about for bearings, trying to find the door.

I felt a weight on my left shoulder, and then a painful compression as if something had taken hold of me. It was not by my choice that I ended up flat on my back, sightless in the dark, fighting, grappling, contacting nothing, while something directly above bore down with a weight that expelled the air from my chest. My very next breath . . . would not come.

I pounded the floor, kicked, screamed without

sound. As consciousness, as life itself, broke away in pieces with the passing seconds, I was lost to panic.

I cannot say, for I do not recall, that I prayed. I cannot say what transaction, if any, may have occurred in the blackening remnants of my consciousness. I can only guess that for whatever reason, the House was satisfied, its message delivered. The weight lifted. Air rushed into my lungs. My reawakened limbs got me to the door, out of that room and into the hall.

The moon had risen, casting precious light through a window at the end of the hall. I thought only of breathing as I labored to my feet, leaning against the wall to support myself. My mind returned with the question of calling for the others—

The very next door burst open and Andi, a dripping, spewing silhouette, tumbled into the hall, rebounded from the opposite wall, and collided with me, coughing, flailing as if drowning. I wrapped my arms around her to bear her up. She spewed water from her mouth and nose, splattering me, the wall, the floor, and I recognized the briny scent, even caught the taste once again, of seawater. She gagged, coughed, gasped for air.

"Easy now," I said, not wanting an explanation, only wanting to calm her, to save her. "Breathe, girl, just breathe."

She calmed, quit flailing as I held her, and with admirable intention drew several wheezing breaths.

"That's it, that's it."

She was dripping wet as if plucked from the sea. Shivering. Her nose was running. Blood from a head wound streaked her face.

She was my employee, but in that moment she

could have been my daughter. I bolted into the room that had nearly smothered me. Defiant, not caring what the House might do, I tore the comforter from the bed and returned, throwing it over Andi's shoulders. She wrapped it around herself, calming, breathing steadily.

"All right?" I asked.

She nodded, willing each breath. "I was in the ocean . . . the whole room was filled with water . . . "

By now I was oxygenated and thinking again. "We'd better check on the others."

We knocked on Brenda's door but didn't wait for the answer we didn't get. We found her flopped on the bed as if lifeless. We shook her, called her name, with no response. I felt the artery in her neck. She was alive but barely breathing. "Let's get her up."

Taking her arms over our shoulders, we bore her from the room. She was limp, nodding off, muttering as if drugged.

"Come on, walk," Andi coached her. "Walk!"

A few feet into the hall, Brenda jerked as if startled. Her legs went to work, bearing her up as her eyes opened and rolled about. "Whaz 'appenin'?" We propped her against the wall. "Whaddaya guys doin'?"

Andi checked her arms. "Look!"

Both arms bore the needle tracks of an addict. The vein in the crook of her left arm bore a needle mark that was recent, red, and swollen.

For an instant I wanted to confront her, rebuke her for such wanton, self-serving, irresponsible—

But then I noticed that Andi's hair, silhouetted in the patch of light at the end of the hall, was wild again. "Excuse me." I reached and felt it. It was dry.

She felt it, then felt her clothing under the

comforter, which prompted her to look once again at Brenda's arms.

The needle tracks were fading.

And so was Brenda's stupor. Her eyes focused. She stroked her arms. "Where'd the guy go?"

"What guy?" asked Andi, her eyes inches from Brenda's.

Brenda recovered further and shook her head. "I was dreaming. Some guy shooting me up . . . " A wave of emotion. She covered her face.

I checked for the wound on Andi's head. It was gone, along with the blood that had streaked her face.

And it was in that moment that I saw beyond her frizzy hair, stark in the moonlight at the end of the hall . . .

A child.

I froze. Brenda and Andi followed my gaze and were as stupefied as I was.

He was a lad of ten years or so, dressed in jeans, untucked shirt, and tennis shoes. His backlit hair glowed like an aura around his head. Despite all our clamor, he didn't seem frightened, but fascinated, studying each of us.

"Please tell me you see that," I whispered. I caught Andi's, then Brenda's eyes. Yes, their faces told me, they saw it too. We looked again—

In that instant of inattention, the lad had vanished. Nothing remained at the end of the hall but an empty patch of moonlight.

And then came the laughter. As if we had become the brunt of a cruel joke, from somewhere came a riotous, mocking laughter, the very stuff of ghost stories and horror movies. We all jumped, quivered. The ladies cowered against the wall, arms protective. I found myself in the center of the hallway, vulnerable on every side and spinning to look for . . . what? Surely not a ghost.

But where was that laughter coming from?

We looked about, narrowed it down . . .

The last door, at the end of the hall. Tank's room.

This was not appropriate, not in keeping with anything we'd experienced. He'd scared years off our lives. What the devil could that big oaf be laughing about at a time like this?

We hurried—I stormed—down the hall to the bedroom door. I rapped on the door so hard I hurt my knuckles.

He was still laughing, whooping, hollering.

I flung the door open and there he stood, enraptured, grinning, wagging his head in wonder as he looked all around the room at—

We saw nothing but a dark bedroom.

"This is so incredible!" he whooped. "Wow! Can you believe this?"

"Believe what?" I asked.

He wagged his head in spellbound wonder. "It is just so beautiful, so perfect!"

His joy made Brenda feel no better. "He's on acid or something."

"Look at that sky!" said Tank. "It just keeps going and going . . . and . . . you hear that music?"

Of course, we didn't.

"Man, can they sing!" Then he sank to his knees in . . . well, a religious moment. "I can see Him! I can see Him standing right there!"

"We need to get him out of here," said Brenda.

"We all need to get out of here," said Andi.

I'd had all the scientific inquiry I could bear for

43

one night. "I heartily agree."

"You can't see this?" Tank was desperate for us to share his experience.

No. We couldn't see it.

"It's heaven! It's gotta be!"

Of course there would be no tearing Tank away from his visions by physical force. We had to talk him back to earth, tell him we were concerned about safety, tired . . .

Scared to the point of a complete emptying of our bowels, Brenda said—I'm paraphrasing.

Tank was elated, satisfied, bolstered in every inch of his being, and that was a lot of inches. He came with us, talking about the flowers, the smells, the music, the joy of the place, the love he saw in "His" face. We got him through the front door and across the street to the woods.

Even in the dark, Van Epps could tell we were out of kilter. "What happened? What did you see?"

"Data we should only discuss by daylight and under calmer circumstances," I insisted.

"I didn't see anything from out here," he said. "I'm afraid I've wasted drive space on—" He went blank, eyes peering across the street.

We turned.

The House was gone.

Chapter 10

A Heated Debriefing

We gathered in the supposed safety of Van Epps' home for the few remaining hours before daylight. We needed sleep, but of course we couldn't get it.

When morning came, our eyes were burning and our nerves were raw. We were in no condition to butt heads over findings and procedures. Tank, wiser than I'd given him credit for, went for a morning jog to depressurize. The rest of us entered into battle, our pointing fingers our swords and coffee cups our shields.

"It's gone," said Van Epps. "And so is the opportunity! The House was yours and you let it get away."

Brenda's crazed eyes and dreadlocks made her a veritable Medusa. "Now listen here, you—" She described him from a library of expletives. "You weren't there! You didn't see it, you didn't feel it, you didn't almost get killed!"

"So where's the data? How do we control this thing? Tell me!"

"Whatcha got on your video besides three hours of static?" To myself and Andi, "Guy can't even run a camera!"

Van Epps came back at me, finger waving. "I did not desert my post!"

Fearing Brenda might round the kitchen table to scratch his eyes out, I intervened. "The data can only be understood by calm and objective minds in the light of day—"

"Oh shut up!" She was just as angry with me. "You were about to piss in your pants, don't give me that super scientist crap!"

"Yes! Yes, I admit being terrified, but that's my point. On a human level—"

She mimicked me, ". . . on a human level . . . "

Disrespect always sets me off. "On a human level we can't trust our impressions because they are skewed by emotion."

Andi—my employee!—jumped in. "But emotions are part of it, they're part of the message. We were supposed to be scared!"

"We are not dealing with a message. We're dealing with an explainable phenomenon, with observations, data, that's all."

"The House was trying to get our attention!"

"Well, see, now you've assigned it some kind of

personality."

Brenda's long fingernail pointed like a weapon. "She didn't assign nothin'! She's right, that thing's talking, and baby, I'm hearing it and you'd better listen too if you want to save your sorry ass!"

Van Epps had a mini-fit in his corner of the room. "So this is the team you brought?"

How dare he? "I didn't bring them!"

He shot a glance at Andi.

I pointed to Brenda. "Well, I didn't bring *her*!"

Brenda slammed down her coffee cup. "That's it, man! I'm outa here!" She addressed Andi on her way to the hall. "This guy ain't human and that's why he's missing the whole point!" She glared at me. "You got as much sense as a refrigerator!"

She was looking for the closet to get her coat. The door she tried was locked. She struck it with her fist.

"Other door," I said.

Andi perked up and went into the hall.

"You're not leaving as well?" I asked.

She ignored me, preoccupied by that locked door.

My cell phone—our phones were the only thing among us recharged—played Beethoven's Fifth. "Yeah?"

"Hey, howdy!"

I was so emphatically, even dangerously *not* in the mood. "What is it?"

He told me but I had to ask him to repeat it. He did.

My world changed.

Brenda was coming out of the hall, headed for the front door. I waved at her to stop. She flipped me off. "It's Tank!" I tried again. "Please, please wait."

Invoking Tank's name worked. She rolled her eyes at the ceiling, but she stopped. Andi was all eyes and ears.

I got a quick report from Tank, found out where he was, and ended the call.

We had to come back from the brink. Hand raised and voice quiet, I said, "All right. We have more data. Now. Calmly, in the daylight, let's agree, please, that we will hear all sides on this." I made eye contact with Brenda. "And that includes me. I will listen to you."

Brenda sniffed in disgust and looked away, but she stayed where she was.

"Andi . . . a word."

I led Andi into the living room, cautioned her to silence, and spoke into her ear. "Have you found any precedents for this, any case of a House . . . carrying messages, as you put it?"

She seemed to be confessing, "No, but—"

"I have some research I need you to do . . . "

Andi went into the kitchen and asked Van Epps for his camera. Van Epps was about to protest, as I expected, but I deftly changed to a more pressing subject. "The House is back. It's right down the street."

That worked. As if everything up to this point, especially our quarrels, was forgotten, we all poured into the street.

I hardly had to direct everyone's attention. I merely looked down the hill and so did they, and we saw the two-story Victorian sitting there as if it had been part of the neighborhood for years.

I expected Van Epps would fly into a seething, four-letter rage, and so he did. So much for logical and practical. This was not the man I once knew, and

48

that seemed to carry a message as much as anything else we were dealing with.

"If you can grant us another chance," I told him, "we'd like to go down there and complete what we couldn't complete last night."

He eased just enough to scold me: "Well, make sure you do!" He waved us on and stormed back into his house. For a moment I saw him pulling back the front blinds to watch.

"Andi, please get that information and join us when you have it." I could see a protest forming and averted it. "It's vital."

She went inside to fire up her computer.

"So where's Tank?" Brenda asked.

"He's in the House, even as we speak."

Chapter 11

Daniel

It was a short walk, during which Brenda and I said not a word to each other. I felt it would be a long time before we did.

Remarkable. The House appeared just as it had the night before: same yard, walkway, planting beds, everything.

Except this time, Tank was standing in the front door, smiling and waving.

I looked at Brenda and she afforded me a cold, wordless return. Even so, by her tentative gait up the walkway I could tell she felt the same, familiar fear as I. We did not like this place.

As for Tank . . . his comfort, his joy with the House was so incongruous as to suggest a meaning of its own.

"Hey, y'all, come on in! I got someone I wantcha to meet!"

Tank turned and went in as if we would follow him.

"Well," I said, "it scared us, but it didn't kill us."

"First time for everything," she responded.

She said something to me. Bolstered, I ventured inside. She followed, giving a closet door a side glance as we passed through the hallway into the kitchen.

Tank had taken a seat at the breakfast table, and there beside him, having a bowl of cereal, was the child. He was dressed in the same untucked shirt and jeans, and now that he was sitting with one foot boyishly askew, I noticed he was missing a sock.

"Everybody, this is Daniel."

The boy looked up at us, munching on his breakfast, expression neutral. I smiled, stumbling over myself to be nonthreatening.

Brenda seemed to have her own issues where a child was concerned. Her cold exterior gave way to an abrupt and inexplicable sorrow that she fought back. At length, she took some deep breaths, then stooped to the boy's level with a smile I'd never seen before. "Daniel, it's great to meet you, baby."

Tank gestured toward an empty chair next to Daniel. "And this is . . . well, I called him Harvey but Daniel didn't like that. So we don't know his name."

Daniel looked up at an invisible someone sitting in that chair, a sizable person judging from his eye line. I looked at the empty chair, at a loss. Nothing was ever going to be normal again, was it?

Tank must have read my face. He laughed, and it was a kind laugh; I took it that way. "Oh, you're all right. I don't see him either. But Daniel does."

Daniel exchanged a smile with the friend who wasn't there.

Brenda asked, "Well . . . is Daniel . . . ?"

Tank reached over and tousled the boy's hair. "Oh yeah. He's real."

Brenda pointed at Tank's tattoo, the one featuring our motley four and this small boy.

Tank shook his head in wonder. "Ain't that wild?" Then he stood. "Hey buddy, we're gonna go into the next room and talk a bit. You just finish up your breakfast, okay?"

The boy gave Tank a smile of complete trust.

Brenda and I went with Tank into the living room, and I noticed how much better I felt. Brenda seemed much more at ease as well. It could have been Tank's carefree and comfortable manner, plus the fact that the living room—indeed, the whole House—was lovely in the daylight, not threatening or mysterious. In any case, I was thinking clearly, and that was indispensable.

We stood in a tight triangle in the finely furnished room.

"Is this the boy you saw last night?" Tank asked.

"He's the one," said Brenda as I nodded.

"I was out jogging, you know, and here he comes running out from between those houses just down the hill, and he's looking scared like somebody's chasing him, and I hollered, 'Hey, bud, you okay?' He acted like he knew who I was because he just came running to me with his arms out, and I picked him up and he put his arms around me and just hung on.

"But—" Tank paused for effect and then wagged his finger to make a point. "I saw two people right on Daniel's tail, and you know what? They were there last night, standing there with the other folks watching the House and watching us."

"A man and a woman?" I asked. "She had short black hair, and he was young, six feet tall, close-cropped hair?"

"Wearing black. Last night and today. They must like black."

"Go on."

"I asked 'em, 'Hey, you want something?' but they just got out of there, didn't say a word." Tank made sure to meet our eyes. "I think they were up to no good. Daniel was scared of 'em, but now they had to deal with me so they took off. Good thing."

"Did Daniel know who they were?"

Tank shrugged. "He didn't say anything . . . which is what he usually does." He hushed his voice and leaned in. "But here's something for you: I was gonna bring him back to Van Epps' place and he wasn't about to go there, either. Looks like he knows that place and he's really scared of it."

"But this place doesn't scare him at all?" Brenda wondered.

"Hey, I tell you what: I was just trying to figure out what to do with him when, bammo, man, here's the House, right here. He dragged me through the front door like he wanted to hide in here, so here we are."

I suggested, "So he's the one who likes peanut butter and jam sandwiches?"

"There's food in the House, stuff that's easy to fix. I guess he's been living here, or hiding here."

"So . . . who is he? Where'd he come from?"

Tank could only shrug. "Guess we could ask him."

We went back into the kitchen. Brenda had the heart, the gentleness to try the direct approach. "Hey, sweetie, we're kind of wondering, just what are you doing here? Do you know why you're here?"

Daniel looked at his invisible friend as if for an answer. Then he directed a long, studying gaze at me and said, "Not yet."

Perhaps it was an answer to Brenda's question. Strangely, I felt it was a message to me.

Chapter 12

One Final Message

"Hello?" came a call from the street.

It was Andi, planted timidly on the pavement. I beckoned from the front door. "Come on in, the coast is clear."

She kept eyeing the House, every step cautious as she came up the front steps and through the doorway. Meeting Daniel helped dispel her fears, though it left her as puzzled as the rest of us.

"What did you find out?" I asked as we four clustered in the living room.

Andi kept her voice low for the child's sake. "I got a report from the assisted living facility. Clyde Morris must have been quite a crumb; they didn't have anything good to say about him. But it's kind of pitiful: They say he died from suffocation. Apparently he rolled over into his pillow and couldn't right himself."

"And Gustav Svensson?"

Andi nodded. "He was a real person, an old fisherman who lived on his boat in the harbor. People say he was a nasty old coot, but he died four days ago." She took a breath, maybe to be sure she still could. "He drowned. But he had a blow to his head. Folks figure he slipped, hit his head, and fell off his boat."

We all met each other's eyes as the pieces came together.

"So," said Brenda, "Mister objective, scientific, poo-poo-the-supernatural-stuff, what do you say now?"

I knew she wanted to corner me. That wasn't about to happen. "Whatever this is . . . it is what it is."

"Oh, that's good, that's real good."

"This is a scientific inquiry. Consequently, even though the means by which we acquire the data is open to question, the data itself could be true. Whatever this is, and however it works, we can't rule out what the House seems . . . to be telling us."

Tank nodded toward the kitchen and young Daniel. "And still is. By the way, his last name is Petrovski. It's written on his shirt collar, and there was a phone number under his name." He handed me a torn corner of paper napkin with the number scrawled on it. I handed it to Andi.

"I'm on it," she said.

"Okay," said Brenda, "So, believing what the

56

House is saying . . . who died from a drug overdose?"

"Or still might?" I said.

She nodded. "We'd better keep an eye on her."

I addressed Andi. "And the files in Van Epps' camera?"

"Three folders, one hour each, nothing but static."

Brenda reiterated, "Guy can't run a camera."

"And there is still . . . " I looked toward the door in the hallway that was locked the night before and, I guessed, still was. "One final message, wouldn't you say?"

Andi and Brenda exchanged a look. They were sisters on this one.

Andi led the way to the door. "Have you seen this before, seen it elsewhere?"

Clearly, we all had.

"Looks just like the same stupid closet door that wasn't the closet door back in Van Epps' place," said Brenda.

I nodded. We were together on this. "You and I both mistook that door for the closet, and both times, it was locked."

"But here it is," said Andi, "a direct copy, and locked just like the other one."

"Hold on," said Tank. He spoke quietly again. "Daniel won't use this hallway. He always goes the long way around, through the dining room, to get to the kitchen."

"We have our next step," I suggested. I was just about to wonder how we might accomplish it when, to our surprise, a lawn mower started up in the front yard.

"What the devil—" I started to say, but was interrupted by the clatter of a chair in the kitchen.

Tank looked, then hurried. "Hey, bud! What's wrong?"

I caught only a glimpse of Daniel before he disappeared, terrified, inside a cupboard and closed the door after him. Tank looked at us, then toward the front door, nonplussed.

Neither I, nor Brenda, nor Andi, had felt comfortable closing the front door behind us, so it remained open, providing a framed view of the front yard. The mower's operator passed across that view, eyes locked ahead of him, a death grip on the mower's handlebar, pushing the mower for all he was worth.

It was A. J. Van Epps.

Chapter 13

The Prison

Data? Van Epps had become an unnerving source of data by his very behavior. He would not stop mowing the lawn even as I chased alongside him, trying to engage him over the roar of the mower.

"Behavioral Analysis!" he shouted to me, turning about and heading back across the lawn again. "We apply an input, such as doing the House a favor, such as mowing the lawn, and see if it triggers a response we can analyze, a change in behavior."

"A change in what behavior?"

He wouldn't answer me. I hurried beside him, almost tripping over the walkway, until I was tired of the game, the indirectness. "What are you afraid of?"

He stopped, but left the mower running, I suppose, to ensure our privacy.

"You can't see it? That thing's a predator, a—a vindicator! It has something against me, against all of us."

I refrained from saying *You're mad!* but I certainly thought it, and I suppose he read it in my face.

"Think what you will, but we—you and I—have become part of the experiment. It intends to take us like the others, and that means practical solutions, direct action."

He continued mowing, leaving me behind. I ran once again to catch up with him and called over the mower. "Do you have any gardening tools? We could help. We could weed the beds, edge the lawn."

That seemed to mollify him, at least for a moment. "In my garage. Help yourself. Please."

I signaled Brenda and Andi to come with me. We agreed with Tank that he should remain with the boy.

In Van Epps' garage we found the tools we needed: a large hammer and a crow bar. Within minutes the obstinate door in Van Epps' hallway splintered away from its lock and creaked open.

It was the doorway to the basement. Steep wooden stairs descended into a musty chamber of web-laced concrete, a nether world of stacks, shelves, and piles of things unneeded and unused.

Directly opposite the base of the stairs was another door, yawning open, hanging crookedly from its hinges. It had been barred shut, but the two-by-four bar had been broken like a toothpick; the door had been locked, but the lock now lay in bent and broken pieces on the concrete, leaving a hole in the door like a shark bite. Strangest of all, the door had been broken *out*, not in, as if a formidable beast had been captive but was now at large.

We found a small room within. There was a bed with its covers askew, and a portable RV toilet. Some toys lay on the floor, some children's books and a box of crayons on the bed. Andi found a single sock, clearly the mate to the one the boy was wearing.

We regarded once again the door that had sealed this room, the concrete walls with no window, the cold, the silence, the prison cell size, and a silence fell over us.

"Friend of yours?" Brenda said at last.

Only to my horror and dismay. It took effort to find my voice. "I . . . cannot defend him."

"Defend him? What for? This is all . . . " She mimicked my voice, my manner. "Entirely pragmatic! A logical step! A practical means to an end!"

"Enough—"

"We'll lock the kid up like a lab rat, purely for the sake of gathering useful data because after all, what are right and wrong but mere social abstractions?"

"You're not being fair—"

"Fair? What do you know about fair?" She waved her hand over the whole mess before us. "I'll tell you *fair*. If I was the House I'd be after him too, and I hope the House gets him!"

She had me on the ropes, but Andi, like the proverbial bell, saved me. "Excuse me? Have you seen this?"

She was referring to strange symbols the boy had scrawled on the wall of the room with a black crayon. It could have been a code, a language, I couldn't tell. I looked to Andi, but she seemed perplexed.

Until I remembered a phrase Van Epps had used: *the handwriting on the wall . . .*

That triggered something in Andi. She gasped, looked at the strange squiggles again, then grabbed a crayon from the bed and began to copy them on the same wall, but in mirror reverse, from left to right. "Oh, no . . ." she said. "Wow. Unreal. It's in script, and he wrote it left to right . . ."

"Keep going, baby," said Brenda.

Andi finished copying, then pointed at the symbols as she read: "May-nay, may-nay, Tay-kel, oo-far-seen."

I now recognized it. "Hebrew."

Andi nodded. "Every Jewish kid learns her Hebrew. This is a quote from—" Then she laughed and wagged her head in wonder. "From the book of Dani'el!"

Brenda was impatient. "So what does it say?"

"Mene," I began. "To count. Tekel: To weigh. Pharsin: to divide."

"The prophet Dani'el's warning to the wicked king Belshazzar," said Andi, her voice hushed with wonder.

"Written by the hand of God on the wall of the king's palace." To Brenda's questioning look I responded, "I was a priest."

Andi explained it. "God was telling Belshazzar, 'Your days are numbered and they've come to an end; You've been weighed in the balance and found wanting; your kingdom is divided among your enemies.'"

"So the boy Daniel has a gift," I mused.

"And one tough dude for a friend," said Brenda,

eyeing the broken door and then pointing to a high basement window still hanging open.

"Harvey?" Andi asked.

Brenda shuddered. "Man, *I* ain't calling him Harvey."

"So as Earthsong told us, he escaped." I recounted the "reading" of the fortune-teller. "A child thought to have a gift . . . he was consulted . . . he was a prisoner, but he broke his bonds and is free and people are looking for him."

Andi eyed the writing on the wall. "God spoke in different ways in the Bible. You know the stories: the burning bush, the donkey that talked to Balaam, Gideon's fleece . . . the hand writing on the wall. I couldn't find a precedent for a 'house holding people accountable,' but maybe the House is another way for God to speak."

"In which case, I'd say Daniel delivered. He spoke for the House, only Van Epps didn't like what he had to say."

"And Daniel isn't the first prophet to be locked up by somebody who didn't like his message," said Andi.

"And Earthsong . . . " Brenda ventured.

I was having the same thoughts. "She knew all about it—and she was careless enough to tell us."

Brenda muttered—maybe a curse—as her hand went to her head.

"What?"

"You okay?" Andi asked.

"You wanted me to tell you if I got any more pictures . . . " Brenda's eyes closed as if viewing something in her mind. "I see . . . blood on the floor."

"Where?" said Andi, looking around.

"In my head!"

"The fortune teller," I said, my guts twisting.

Their eyes asked for an explanation.

"Your comments, Brenda, about Van Epps being unable to run a camera. We can say for sure he was minding that camera long enough to record three hours of static."

"But—" said Andi, eyes widening.

"Exactly," I said. "We were in the House for five."

Chapter 14

The Third Death

I assigned Andi to a safe and neutral position behind a tree on a small bluff overlooking the House and, just up the street, Van Epps' home. She was not to approach either one—which was fine with her—but to let us know if anything developed. In the meantime, she could follow up on the phone number Tank found on Daniel's shirt collar.

Brenda and I returned by back roads to Earthsong's Psychic Readings to find a CLOSED sign hanging in the window. We knocked, we called out, we got no response. Brenda drew upon her street wisdom, gained admittance through a side window, and let me in through the front door.

Upstairs, a sound system was playing psychedelic rock from the sixties. We ventured up the stairs to the living quarters, a dimly lit, cultural throwback with tie-dyed tapestries, black light posters of Morrison, Hendrix, and Joplin, walls randomly splattered in pop art colors.

We found Earthsong on her bed, two fresh needle marks in her arm, the syringe on the nightstand. She had nodded off and fallen into a deeper and deeper sleep until she was dead.

"Don't touch anything," I cautioned.

"So here's death number three," said Brenda.

"Murder number three, I'm afraid." I used a pen from my pocket to press the sound system's *off* button and immediately confirmed the stirrings I thought I'd heard downstairs.

I went to the top of the stairs and called out, "Lady and Gentleman, she's dead and we are witnesses; we have the child in our custody, and Van Epps will be convicted of murder. Now you can kill us and draw all the more attention, or you can abandon Van Epps right here, right now, and slink back under your secretive rock to fight another day."

Brenda, beside me, was clearly surprised to hear footfalls move through the building. We caught only the back of the man and woman going out the front door.

"Our error, leaving that door unlocked," I said. "They've been following us from the beginning. We've seen them before: scum from that Institute, damage controllers, trying to find Daniel and letting Van Epps know our every move—beginning with our visit to this very place. Earthsong thought you and I were them. That's why she showed off so much—and said things she shouldn't have."

"And Van Epps killed her?"

I felt condemned by my own concession. "As you reminded me, it was the pragmatic, logical, practical thing to do. She was his mistress, which explains how she knew about Daniel, his gift, how Van Epps held him prisoner, and how he escaped. And being Van Epps' mistress, of course she'd be jealous when Van Epps brought in Daniel to consult instead of her. So she was jealous of Daniel and high on heroin, which made her blabby, a liability. If she mouthed off so freely to you and me, who else might she talk to?

"You noticed there were two needle marks? The first dose was administered by Earthsong to satisfy her addiction; the second fatal dose was administered by her lover who knew where she kept her heroin— who no doubt supplied it in the first place, in exchange for sexual favors. He was only minding his camera outside the House for three of the five hours we were inside. The other two afforded him the opportunity to come here, eliminate the risk of discovery, and return to meet us outside the House, his jacket freshly imbued with more of Earthsong's incense, by the way.

"As for Clyde Morris and Gustav Svensson, if we believe the pattern set by the House—which logic, not belief, compels me to do—it follows that the same person who engineered Earthsong's death is also responsible for the other two." I reached for my cell phone. "I would say it's time to call the police."

In my hand, my cell phone played Beethoven's Fifth. The screen told me it was Andi. "Yes?"

She was so frantic I could barely understand her.

"Van Epps! He's trying to burn the House down,

and Tank and Daniel are still inside!"

Chapter 15

A House Afire

At perilous speed we drove back to where the House . . . used to be. At that location we found a field overtaken by blackberries.

Up the street, directly across from Van Epps' home, the House stood rock solid even as smoke poured from the windows and flames licked about the porch. The can of gasoline for the mower lay on its side in the front yard, emptied. Van Epps was just coming from his garage with another can and some empty beer bottles.

Andi ran to us as we screeched to a halt and burst from the car. "Tank and Daniel are inside!"

Before I could get to him, Van Epps hurled a gasoline-filled bottle through the front window. An explosion of new flames followed, roiling and engulfing the living room, the walls, the furniture.

I ran and stood between him and the House. "Are you out of your mind? Stop this!"

As if I were not even there, he raged against the burning building. "Come after me, will you? How do *you* like burning? I'll send you back where you came from, you filthy—"

He grabbed another bottle and would have filled it, but I blocked the action and the bottle shattered on the street. "A. J., come to your senses! Look at what you've become!"

For the first time he looked at me. "Become? *Become?* This *is* me, James! I am what I've always been, and this—" he indicated his arsenal of gasoline and bottles—"this is survival!"

The ladies were screaming for Tank and Daniel. The House was becoming an inferno, the flames roaring up the sides, black smoke venting out the eaves.

A chair crashed through an upstairs window, followed by a huge, smoking body. Tank! He plunged, rolled down the porch roof, took hold of a trellis as he pitched over the edge, and grabbed the autumn-deadened branches of a vine to break his fall. He landed and collapsed on the lawn, rolling in the grass to extinguish flames which, I saw, I hoped, had not ignited on him. I and the ladies were there instantly, checking him over.

He was blackened by smoke and soot, bleeding from scrapes and cuts, wracked with coughing, fighting for life. Yet still he managed to cry, "Daniel!

70

Daniel!"

Flames were shooting out the window he'd just come through. Daniel. Oh, child! No one could still be alive in there.

Andi shrieked, "Daniel!"

I followed her horrified gaze across the street.

Daniel! There he was, crossing the street, hand in hand with he-whom-we-were-not-to-call-Harvey . . . heading for Van Epps' front door.

"He made it, he made it!" Brenda shouted to Tank.

Daniel met our eyes, our horror, with a look of such peace, I felt all reason leave me. Child, what are you doing?

Van Epps caught sight of Daniel even as the boy went in his front door. Van Epps abandoned his pyromania and dashed toward his house, bounded up his stairs, burst through the doorway.

No! Oh dear God, no!

Tank was fallen, barely turned from the brink of death. The ladies were tending to him and hadn't the strength . . .

And for reasons only the heart, not the mind, can know, I ran for that door.

Chapter 16

The Monster

I bounded up the stairs two at a time. In one blurred moment I crossed the porch and burst through the front door—

And into a cage with a monster.

Van Epps held Daniel in a desperate grip, and a knife to Daniel's throat. "Stop right there, James!"

I stopped. I raised my hands. "A. J. This is—you must admit—highly irregular."

"But *you* must admit, entirely pragmatic!" His crazed eyes locked on the burning House; the glow of the fire played on his face. "A life for a life. I'm sure the House understands the concept!"

"It would only be another murder!"

"Murder?" He actually laughed. "Am I talking to James McKinney? Since when did murder become more than a social concept? Since when did you decide to be a hero?"

I was struck dumb. What could I say, where could I go from here?

Van Epps was enjoying the upper hand. "Morris was a drunken, wife-beating wretch and deserved to die anyway. All I did was control the time of death."

To my own indictment, I understood his reasoning. "Controlling the conditions for observing the phenomena."

"And it worked: it produced a posthumous sighting and photographs of Clyde Morris; the House appeared again; we got the account from Morris' widow."

"So what about Gustav Svensson?"

"A blight on the face of the town! Constantly soiling the tourists' experience with his foul temperament. Hated! So, we needed observable, repeatable results. I took the necessary steps—and we got them."

I erred in taking a step forward. His knife went anew to Daniel's throat. "Easy! Easy!"

I took a step back.

The knife stayed right where it was. "So don't you see, James? Repeatable results mean predictability, and predictability means eventual control. Had we understood the House, we could have controlled it. We could have harnessed it."

"*And* turned it aside?"

His glare was condemning. "Exactly."

I grimaced. A monster being reasonable. Another monster would have accepted his argument. I, at least, saw the logic in it. I felt sick.

"I suppose," I ventured, "Earthsong was only a complication?"

"She . . . and the kid." He waved the knife under Daniel's nose.

"He only delivered the message, A. J. Locking him up didn't change anything and killing him certainly won't."

"His life for mine, James. Behavioral control of that thing over there . . . until it burns to the ground."

"Not at such a cost! Never."

As if to confirm my words, there came a rumbling in the floor, in the walls, and then a shaking so severe the furniture danced. We fell. Daniel wriggled free. The noise shook my insides. Dishes, lamps, books showered down and I felt I was riding the floor, fists clenching wads of carpet, as it heaved and bucked and the room spun about. Where was Daniel?

I saw the knife, fallen from Van Epps' hand and jittering upon the floor. I knew he would go for it, so I did. We collided in the center of the room, neither of us procuring the knife, both of us reduced to a savage brawl: rolling, kicking, striking—I even bit his hand. The degradation was appalling and my skills as a grappler non-existent, but there we were, rabid animals in a huge tumbler, trying to kill each other.

Somehow Van Epps got hold of me from behind, and as he compressed my throat and I fought for life, an infinitesimal part of my awareness took note of four facts: the room had changed, my friends were shouting and pounding on the front door, Daniel stood safely in a corner, watching, and . . . Daniel was also watching someone else, his eyes expectant.

Suddenly, Van Epps let out an *oof*, released me, and I tottered forward, turning in time to see him slam against the wall. That I would have such strength surprised me.

The advantage, however, was now his. He had the knife again and charged like a raging bull. I may have ducked when he thrust the knife. I only remember tumbling onto the couch while he went flying over it and then let out a cry.

I leaped from the couch, eyes everywhere, not seeing him—

A groan came from the archway between the living and dining rooms. The couch blocked my view, but as I rounded it I found my adversary fallen, a pool of crimson spreading beneath him, the knife up to the hilt between his ribs.

Only then, as I gasped for breath, did I realize the tumult and quaking had ceased. Only then did I recognize the dining room with its eight place settings and high-backed chairs. I was standing in the House. Except for the disarray I and Van Epps had caused, no harm was done, and not the slightest scent of smoke remained.

As if by the House's will, the front lock released, the door burst open, and in spilled Tank, Andi, and Brenda. Tank was scorched and tattered, but ready to . . . well, I suppose I beat him to it.

Aghast, they took in the scene, from Daniel safe in the corner to the upset furniture to the body of Van Epps, unquestionably dead. Brenda stared in recognition at the pool of blood on the floor, then at me.

"Duly noted," I replied.

"You're bleeding!" Andi cried.

Oh. A cut on my hand. Nothing deep or serious, but sufficiently dramatic. Even so, something else warranted my attention: an awareness, an urgency. "Get Daniel out of here."

"But—"

"Tank, if you would, please."

Tank hurried over and scooped Daniel up.

I could not say how I knew and there wasn't time to sort it out. "It isn't over. Get out. Now."

Oh, the cacophony of voices, the static!

"What?"

"What are you talking about?"

"How do you know?"

"I just *do*, for God's sake . . . pardon the term!" The House shook, a familiar sensation. "Go!"

I shoved and herded them, surprised at my strength, ashamed of my manners, and got them through the door. The latch fell into place and I caught my breath.

The quiet brought no comfort; a lull before a storm. Once again, I was afraid.

I felt a chill behind me and turned.

There stood Van Epps, ghostly white, eyes pasty, blood streaking his clothes, the knife in his hand.

Chapter 17

A Hero

The knife came down, I dodged it. Van Epps lunged
for me; I leaped, tumbled over the back of the couch,
got to my feet, and ran across the room—where he
met me, plunging the knife again. I dodged again, and
must have struck him with an elbow—he took a
blow, jerking sideways, off balance. I put out my foot
to kick him but missed; he fell anyway. When he came
at me again I had a lamp in my hands, but didn't have
to swing it. Inches from me, his body and face
flattened as if he'd struck a thick pane of glass

between us. He fell back and nearly tripped over something.

It was his own body, dead on the floor, the knife protruding.

From his guttural gasp and the way he wilted, I had a fair idea the fight was over. He teetered there, gawking, horror stretching his veiny face, a ghostly copy of himself, complete with a blood-stained knife. He dropped the knife—it dissolved before touching the floor—looked at me, looked at himself . . . then around the room.

His silence spoke though he could not. No arguments remained, no rationales. I could see he knew.

The House had him.

And as quick as that thought, three guests appeared, seated at the dining table: Clyde Morris, hunched and worn, resigned to his fate; Gustav Svensson, bitterness tightening his face, eyes glaring; Earthsong, her beauty fading even as she sat there, her eyes showing the wounds of betrayal.

I could not, I dared not move or speak. I could only hope, foolishly, that they could not see me, that I wasn't really standing in the same room, the same House, with the man now facing his accusers.

Van Epps and I had long assured and supported each other in our opinions. We had mocked those who believed in a God and any day of reckoning. In anger, in bitterness, I had killed God long ago and ever after wished Him dead. Though all appearances suggested it was Van Epps on trial, was I not partly responsible for his being there?

Clyde Morris seemed interested only in Van Epps as he produced a pillow, Van Epps' instrument of murder, and laid it on the table.

Gustav Svensson followed, producing a blood-stained rock.

Earthsong, saddened, produced the syringe used to kill her and set it beside the pillow and the rock.

Van Epps didn't speak. What was there to say?

A door in the hall answered, its hinges creaking, and immediately a wind moved through the House, swaying and jingling the chandelier, rustling the curtains. Van Epps' eyes rolled toward the hallway as if he knew what the sound was; the three accusers simply turned their heads; they already knew what it was.

True to the widow Morris' account, a powerful body of air hit me in the back and sent me reeling in the direction of the hall. Van Epps, caught in the same rush of air, stumbled and staggered ahead of me, arms fighting off flying newspapers, serviettes, doilies, a tablecloth, any and all things the wind could carry. I grasped a dining room chair but it only came with me. I could hear Van Epps screaming over the gale.

Just ahead of me, the three accusers, Morris, Svensson, and Earthsong, walked into the hallway even as their images dissolved into particles like sand before the wind. The doorway—yes, the House's precise copy of Van Epps' basement door—stood gaping, the glow of a furnace pulsating upon the opposite wall. Like specks of dust drawn into a vacuum, what was left of the three shot through.

Van Epps dropped to the floor, grabbed for the carpet, a server, a hutch, to no avail as the wind carried him—and me—toward that door. I could feel the heat.

It was not a thought, for there wasn't time. It was a knowledge: I'd been on trial with Van Epps. Hope as I might, argue as I might, the House was good with its promise: it knew all about me.

Van Epps blurred through the door with a shriek. The rectangular frame of fire filled my vision, I flew helplessly, headlong—

My body slammed against an unseen barrier stretched across the door and I hung there, a gale force pulling my arms, legs, coat tails and hair into the throat of a flaming, roaring tunnel. Far ahead of me, Van Epps, a rag doll in silhouette, tumbled, kicked, screamed, shrank into oblivion.

How might I escape? How? I looked away from the fiery maw that would swallow me, desperate to know my situation. What held me here? How might I work my way to safety?

Only in that tiny and panicked measure of time did I realize my body had come up against another—I felt the shape of a powerful chest against mine and, on further groping for escape, I discerned what could have been huge arms. I looked up.

I saw the glow of the fire on the lintel of the door, the wall, and the ceiling above, but somehow, in the light of the flames and the shadows cast, I saw the outline of a face: the shape of a jaw, a brow, the crown of a head. Although I could not see the eyes plainly, I could feel them watching me. I looked where I knew them to be, and . . .

I could not plead. No words would come.

The huge arm to my left reached out; the door swung shut with a clamorous *bang!*

And I came to my senses on the floor, my body in a heap against the basement door in the home of the late A. J. Van Epps. His body still lay where it fell, a dim and crumpled shadow against the sweep of red and blue lights that came through the front windows.

Chapter 18

Reflection

The fire crew grumbled a little, trying to understand why they'd been called to a fire when now, search as they might, there was none to be found. There wasn't even a burning House to be found, only an old field with a long defunct chicken coop. I think some of them knew, but they weren't going to say anything.

The police had plenty to do, stretching their yellow ribbon around Van Epps' home and beginning the long process of piecing together his death, his basement prison, the prisoner, and three murders.

According to their instructions, I waited with my friends on the front steps, shakily sipping from a cup of water. Along with our debriefing each other, we discussed lodging; getting everything explained was going to take a while.

Faithful Andi reported, "The phone number on Daniel's shirt got me the Norquist Center for Behavioral Health—it's a home for the insane. They've been looking for Daniel. Daniel's uncle and aunt came to take him for a few days but never brought him back, and as it turns out, they weren't his real uncle and aunt."

I nodded, theorizing. "Our charming couple from that Institute, no doubt. Van Epps had friends he wouldn't talk about—friends wanting 'power.'"

Brenda draped a blanket over my shoulders. "I'll bet they were tracking little Daniel the same as they were tracking me and Tank for our 'special gifts.'"

"And brought him here to help them . . . what? Make contact with the House? Well, what he provided was not to Van Epps' liking."

"Hey," said Tank, "it was God talking. You want to hear from God, you better be ready for the truth."

God. So many issues there. Such a long history. Such a long, long journey back should I even desire to make it. I didn't care to rebut Tank's faith, not today. I only asked him, for the record, "Did you really see heaven?"

Tank grinned. "Jesus was there. It couldn't have been anything else." Then with a sober, thoughtful air he added, "The House only tells the truth. For some it's good news; for others . . . "

Brenda put an arm around Daniel and drew him close. "I'll tell you something. Daniel's not insane.

He's like anybody else folks don't understand."

I reached and touched the boy's cheek. "I'm glad you're all right, son." Then I added with a wink, "That's quite a protector you have."

Daniel replied, "Yes, sir," and smiled up at his invisible friend.

"So what do you suppose, Daniel? You heard the House's message. You wrote it on the wall. Did the House take Dr. Van Epps because he killed those people and almost killed you?"

"No, sir."

We waited for more.

"The House took him because he was the kind of person who would."

I could still see myself hanging in that doorway. There, but for the grace of God . . .

"It could have been me."

I saw the same look I'd seen in Daniel's eyes the last time he said it: "Not yet."

FROM HARBINGERS 3
THE SENTINELS

ANGELA HUNT

I was sitting on the edge of my grandparents' deck, bare legs swinging in the sun, when Abby trotted out of the house and sat beside me. "Abs!" I slipped my arm around her back and gave her a hug; she returned my affection by licking my cheek. "Stop that, silly. You know I'm ticklish."

As if she understood, Abby straightened and joined me in staring out at the sea oats and the white sandy beaches of the Gulf of Mexico. We had sat in this same spot hundreds of times in our growing-up years . . . me, the geeky high-schooler, and Abby, the ungainly Labrador pup. Somehow we had both outgrown our awkwardness.

I ran my head over the back of her head, then scratched between her ears. My heart welled with nostalgia as tears stung my eyes. "I've missed you, Abs," I whispered. "All that time away at college . . . I wish you could have been with me. Maybe I wouldn't have been so homesick if you were there."

She whimpered in commiseration, then gave me another kiss.

My throat tightened at the thought of eventually losing her. Big dogs tended to have shorter lifespans, and all the books said Labs lived an average of twelve to fourteen years. Which meant I'd only have my girl for another five or so years . . . I had to get home more often.

Abby pricked up her ears, then pulled away from me and jogged down the deck steps.

"Abs! You know you're not supposed to go down to the beach."

When it suited her, Abby had selective hearing. Pretending not to hear me, she dove into the bed of sea oats. I couldn't see her in the thick undergrowth, but the tasseled heads of the stalks bent and trembled as she passed by.

"You're going to get sand spurs in your coat!"

No answer but the rustle and crunch of dry vegetation. Then a warning bark, followed by a throaty growl.

She had probably found a rat, but for some reason her growl lifted the hairs on my arm. I stood and walked to a better vantage point, hoping to spot her. "Abby!" I brightened my voice. "Want a treat? A cookie?"

Another bark, and then a sharp yelp, followed by a frenzy of rustling and crunching. Then Abby began to cry in a constant whine as she retraced her steps, moving faster this time. Had she found a snake? Venomous snakes were not common on the beach, but this was Florida . . .

I flew down the stairs, drawn by the urgency in her tone. "Abs! Come here, honey. Come on, baby, come on out."

If she'd been bitten, I had only minutes to get her to a vet. My grandparents had left a car in the garage, keys on the ring by the door . . .

Abby appeared in the pathway. She lifted her head for an instant and wriggled her nose, parsing the air for my scent. Then she ran to me, barreling into my legs and knocking me onto the sand.

"Abs?" She was on top of me, thrashing her head while she whined, and with great difficulty I managed to catch her jowls. "Abby-girl, let me look—"

My breath caught in my throat. Abby's panicked breaths fluttered over my face as I stared into what had once been gentle brown eyes but were now empty, blood-encrusted caverns.

Everything went silent within me, and I screamed.

SELECTED BOOKS BY
FRANK PERETTI

Illusion: A Novel
This Present Darkness
Piercing the Darkness
The Oath
Prophet
Tilly
The Visitation
Monster

Web page: www.frankperetti.com

Facebook:
https://www.facebook.com/officialfrankperetti

Don't miss the other books in the Harbingers series:

The Girl, by **Alton Gansky**.

The Sentinels, **by Angela Hunt.**

CPSIA information can be obtained at www.ICGtesting.com
Printed in the USA
LVOW10s2158240816

501735LV00014B/290/P